It was a dark and stormy night ...

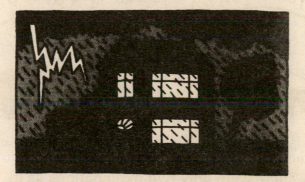

   Just the sort of night to curl up on the sofa
and watch my favourite horror video, *I Was
Frankenstein's Monster's Vampire Werewolf.*
Exactly the sort of night, in fact, that you
might have read about in *How To Handle
Your Brother*[1]. This is hardly surprising, as it
was the same night.

1: To read *How To Handle Your Brother*, either stay sitting where you are,
turn to the back of the book, then turn it the other way up, or turn to the
back of the book, keep it the same way up and stand on your head. If you
are already standing on your head, you can perhaps sense a strange
rush ... standing on your head. Unless
you ... ... case it's water
rus ...

I'd gone out to the back room to get my *I Was Frankenstein's Monster's Vampire Werewolf* video from my little brother, but when I returned to the front room, the telly had disappeared.

"Yahhhhh!!!" I yelled, baring my soul in fury. "Yahhhhh!!!" yelled my video, baring its teeth in fury.

This was only to be expected; it was a vampire werewolf video, after all.

There were only two explanations as to the telly's disappearance. 1: it had been taken by a bug-eyed alien from the Planet Zlot known as Mygitrod, or 2: it had been taken by a bug-eyed alien from the upstairs back bedroom better known as my big sister.

Mygitrod   My Big Sister

I hammered on her bedroom door. "Bring that telly back downstairs," I shouted. But I couldn't make myself heard above the sound of swearing, fighting, smashing glasses and breaking windows.

My sister was watching *EastEnders*. Just what kind of Joker did she think she was? I went out to the stables to talk to the only real friend I had: my old nag Dobbin[1]. He was watching the Australian soap opera that's a favourite with horses everywhere – *Neigh-Bores*.

Aw strewth Joelene!

"What am I going to do about that little toerag of a sister of mine, Dobbin?" I asked him. "Fancy nicking the telly! She really does think she's a Joker. The little brat!"

1: I do have another old nag, of course – my big sister.

"I used to have the same trouble with my sister," said Dobbin.

"Was she a little fool, too?" I asked.

"No," replied Dobbin, "she was a little *foal*."

"Come on, Dobbin," I said. "The good people of Coffsweet City need us. Their lives are being made a misery by the antics of the Brats a.k.a. sisters."

As we swooped over the skyscrapers, people called out:

"Is it a plane?"

And...

"Is it a bird?"

Which just shows you how thick they were, mistaking a boy on a horse for a jumbo jet or a pigeon. Suddenly:

"It's BRATMAN!" went up the cry.

"I have come to teach you how to handle your sisters!" I announced.

"Whizzo!" they said. "Our sisters are driving us crazy!"

"Then there is no time to lose!" I declared.

"What shall we do first, Bratman?" asked the people.

"Turn the page over, of course!" I replied.

Scholastic Children's Books,
Commonwealth House, 1-19 New Oxford Street,
London WC1A 1NU, UK
a division of Scholastic Ltd
London ~ New York ~ Toronto ~ Sydney ~ Auckland

Published in the UK by Scholastic Ltd, 1998

ISBN 0 590 19684 7

Typeset by Rapid Reprographics
Printed by Cox & Wyman Ltd, Reading, Berks.

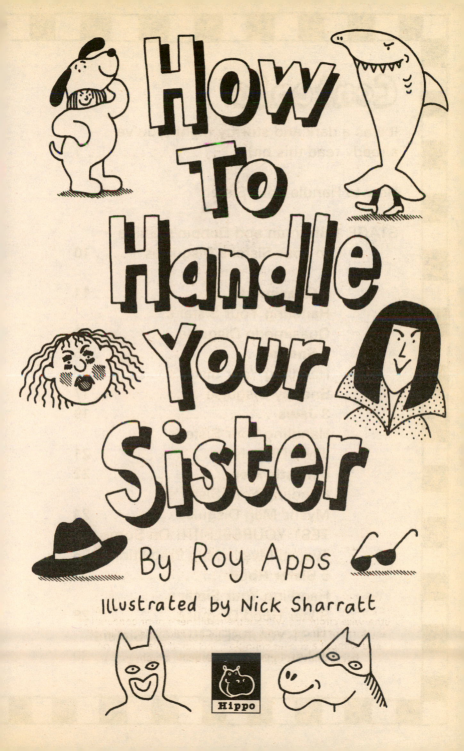

How To Handle Your Sister

By Roy Apps

Illustrated by Nick Sharratt

Contents

How To Handle Your Sister : Stage One

Just like the Joker[1], sisters have the power to take on various disguises. These are likely to be related to their favourite films and telly shows. This has the obvious advantage that you don't have to see what they really look like, which can be pretty gruesome, or rather not-so-pretty gruesome. But Bratman and Dobbin's Guide to Your Sister's Disguises will enable you to know instantly just what she's up to, so that you can turn the tables on her.

Alternatively, if you're not into ruining your mum's best dinner service, use the guide to turn your sister's disguises to your own advantage.

1: And for that matter, brothers (see *How To Handle Your Brother* page 10).

BRATMAN AND DOBBIN'S GUIDE TO YOUR SISTER'S DISGUISES

Sister Disguise 1: **Quasimodo**

Dobbin and I plodded through Coffsweet City's more than forbidding streets. Then we turned into a street that was less than forbidding. It was three-bidding. I knocked at the door of a small, terraced house. The door was opened by Kerry. Kerry Onlarfing, that is.

"Bratman! Thank goodness you've come!" said Kerry. "My sister's up to something." "You'd better explain," I said.

Kerry took me to the upstairs landing. "For days now, everything in our house has been quiet," said Kerry. "My sister's kept herself to herself, leaving an empty tray outside her bedroom door after each mealtime. What's going on, Bratman?"

Before I could answer, Kerry's sister's bedroom door was flung open and an appalling creature stood before us.

"Aaargh!" I said.

"Sister dear, you look dreadful! Can I get you something?" enquired Kerry, being a caring and sensitive sort of sister. "Something like a new face?"

Luckily I pulled Kerry out of the way just in time, otherwise she would have ended up looking just like her sister – i.e. a total wreck.

Kerry tried another tack. "Sister dear, you look dreadful! Have you been unwell?" she asked.

Once again, I had to drag Kerry out of the range of her sister's fists.

Quickly, I explained a few things to Kerry. "Your sister has given herself a Joker-type Quasimodo disguise.

"She's spent *days* getting herself to look like this. She thinks she looks cool. She thinks she looks stunning. She thinks she'll turn a few heads, especially the head of Coffsweet City High School Year Twelve heartthrob, Henry Hunk. Of course, rather than turning a few heads, she's more likely to turn a few stomachs."

Kerry's face dropped. So I picked it up for her.

"What ever shall I do, Bratman?"

Handling Your Sister's Quasimodo Disguise:

Put my blinkers on for a start!

"The best way to handle your sister's Quasimodo disguise," I explained, "is Aversion Therapy. People use this to get over their fear of spiders or flying. However, I have a fear of Aversion Therapy, so I use Another Version therapy. This is the way it works. You toughen yourself up by looking at pictures of the faces of all sorts of hideous monsters, so that when you actually see your sister in her Quasimodo disguise, she doesn't look quite as bad as before."

To help Kerry, I showed her some particularly gruesome examples... You can have a look too, if you dare.

Joe Nassaw's sister: Di Nassaw

Darren Stee's sister: Bea Stee

Dean Fying-Monster's sister: Terri Fying-Monster

"Once you have learnt to look upon your sister's face without freezing in terror every time, you will find her dead useful," I continued.

Indeed, a few weeks later I got a letter from Kerry Onlarfing. This is what it said:

> Dear Bratman,
> Yesterday I went to Burger Bar. I knew it would be difficult to get a seat, so I took my sister. As soon as all the other customers saw her, they fled! Leaving us free to take the best table by the window.
> Thank you, Bratman!
> Lots of love
> Kerry xxx

Sister Disguise 2: **Snoopy**

When I arrived at Harriet Toomuchpudding's house, I found she had a grim story to tell.

"It happened last week," she began. "I was on the phone to my best friend Kate about her birthday party. 'Is your cousin going to be there?' I asked her.

And she said, 'Sebastian, you mean?'

'Yeah,' I said. 'Hey, you won't tell anyone this will you...?'

'Tell them what?' Kate said.

'Tell them that I think Sebastian's like a raspberry milk shake with ten sugar lumps in it.'

'Eh?' Kate said.

'He's rather sweet!' I whispered.

"Suddenly I became aware of a little puppy dog nuzzling its ear to the phone. 'He-hee!' giggled this puppy dog. 'He's rather sweet! He's rather sweet!'

"Then I realized something: this dog thought it was a parrot! 'Good girl! Sit down! I'll fetch you a bone in a minute,' I said to the dog.

"Then I realized something else: we haven't got a dog that thinks it's a parrot. We haven't even got a dog that thinks it's a dog!"

"This is serious," I said. "Do you know who the dog was?"

Harriet shook her head.

"It was your little sister, in her Joker-type Snoopy disguise."

"But Snoopy's a lovable little cartoon pup!" protested Harriet.

"Ha! That's the cunning of it," I said. "When little sisters take on Joker-type Snoopy disguises, they turn not into sweet-faced little pets with large, floppy ears, but suet-faced little pests with large, stroppy ears."

I'd hardly finished, when I saw Harriet racing out of the room.

"Where are you going?" I asked.

"To wipe that smile off my sister's face," she replied.

"I appreciate that's a very tempting thing to do, particularly for a sensitive, caring sister like yourself," I said, "but why waste a perfectly good dishcloth?"

"Have you a better suggestion, then?" Harriet asked.

"I have," I said.

"Oh gee, thanks!" said Harriet.

Handling Your Sister's Snoopy Disguise:

What about me?

"Oh Gee-gee, thanks!" said Harriet.

"To handle your sister's Snoopy disguise successfully requires crafty guile and cunning," I warned.

"I don't know any crafty guiles," said Harriet sadly.

"Don't worry, a crafty boy will do just as well," I reassured her. "What you need to do is to fill in the gaps in the letter on the next page, then cut it out and leave it in a place your sister is bound to look: i.e. your pencil case marked TOP SECRET, FOR MY EYES ONLY or the freezer compartment marked TOP SECRET, FOR MY ICE ONLY."

Dear ....[1]

I am very sorry, but I won't be able to come to your birthday party next ....
   She doesn't know this, but my dear little sister is being sent to a clinic in Outer Mongolia for specialist medical treatment. It's her ears, you see. She's spent so much time listening at key holes and half-open doors, that her ears have been affected. Unless she has this treatment, in a few weeks her ears will be the size of giant cabbages.
   Of course Outer Mongolia is a long trek, but I'm told the pack-horses are very reliable. It's the only place in the world where they do this special operation because of the particular species of leeches found there, but it's still a pity there's no anaesthetic available.
   Of course, if she was to stop snooping, the operation might not become necessary.
   Don't breathe a word of this to anyone. Mum and Dad have not told my sister anything for fear of causing her distress.
Your friend

....[2]

1: Write your friend's name here.
2: Write your name here.

Sister Disguise 3: **Jaws**

After all my hard work, I decided it was time
to take a well-earned break at the Coffsweet
City Leisure Centre.

I went through to the swimming pool.
Dobbin wanted to come too, but
unfortunately there was a sign which said:

NO HORSE PLAY

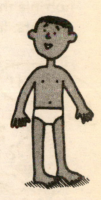

"This looks a nice
pool," I said to the
boy standing next to
me. He nodded.
"My name's Bratman,
by the way."
"Oh, hello Bratman-
by-the-way,
my name's Toby."
"Would that be Toby Ornotobe?"
He nodded. He was about to jump in when
he saw something in the water. Something
that sent a shiver down his spine.
Something that said: "Don't forget, Toby,
Mummy says you mustn't go in without your
Quacky Duck armbands on!"
Toby went as white as a sheet and fled
into the changing rooms.

I knew what he had seen in the water. His little sister in a Joker-type Jaws disguise. You know the film, of course: just when you thought it was safe to go back into the water... Eieieie!!!! a horrible thing with a wicked toothy grin appears. It's a shark!

This is how a sister's Jaws disguise works: just when you thought it was safe to go into the swimming pool and show your mates how good you are at dive-bombing, a horrible thing with a wicked toothy grin appears. It's your little sister.

After my swim, as I sat in the coffee bar, Toby came up with his mates. "What am I going to do, Bratman?" he asked.

"Let me think about this one," I replied. "You go off with your mates on your bike."

"Thanks, Bratman, I will," he said.

But no sooner had he got to the door, than a dreadful sight confronted him.

"I'm coming with you, Toby! I've got my twinkie bike outside!" It was Toby's little sister.

"Aaargh!" said Toby. "What shall I do, Bratman!? What shall I do?"

I had no answer.

Handling Your Sister's Jaws Disguise:

"What do you say, Dobbin?" asked Toby desperately.

"He's right," I said. "Jump on!"

It's the only thing to do I'm afraid, if your little sister dons her Joker-type Jaws disguise.

Clip, clop, clip, clop...

RUN FOR IT!!!!!!!!!!!!!!!!!!!!!!!

You're bound to be able to run faster than her. Even Dobbin could run faster than Toby's little sister.

Sister Disguise 4: **Mystic Meg**

I sat in Rosie Cheeks' house, in a dingy part of Coffsweet City.

"I'm having real problems with my sister," she sighed. "What kind of problems?" I asked. "She's being a real **********," replied Rosie.[1]

Suddenly a face leered round the door. What a surprise! It was Mystic Meg, the famous astrologer who knows everything that's going to happen. "You know what will happen if you keep saying that word, don't you?" she asked Rosie.

"Can't say I do," replied Rosie.

"Your tongue will drop off."

1: This is a word that's too rude to print (see *How To Handle Your Brother* page 44).

Then a thought
suddenly struck me.
"Yee-oww!!"
After I'd picked
myself up and rubbed
the bruise on my head,
I realized something.
That leering face didn't
belong to Mystic Meg!

That fact meant one of only two things.

Either:

1 Mystic Meg was a member of the Sister
Hood[1] and had stolen the face in question.
or

2 It wasn't Mystic Meg at all, but Rosie's
sister in her Joker-type Mystic Meg disguise.
Chances were, I guessed,
that it would be 2.
"It's your sister,
Rosie! In her
Joker-type
Mystic Meg
disguise,"
I shouted.

1: See page 27.

"What!" said Rosie. She turned to her sister. "On your bike[1], you great *******!"

"You know what will happen if you keep saying that word, don't you?" said her sister.

"Can't say I do," said Rosie.

"Rosie! Stop it! Or else you'll end up having the same conversation for what seems like eternity."[2]

"What shall I do then, Bratman?" asked Rosie.

Handling Your Sister's Mystic Meg Disguise:

Dobbin says:

Dinner, dinner, dinner, dinner, Bratman!

Fill up my nosebag, would you please?

I said, "Just wait until I've instructed Rosie on how to handle her sister's Mystic Meg disguise, will you?"

Quickly, I explained to Rosie what she had to do. And this is what happened.

1: Don't, whatever you do, say this if your sister is also prone to putting on the Sister Hood disguise. Because if she is, it will be *your* bike she gets on.

2: Or as long as it takes your big sister to get out of the bathroom in the morning – whichever is the longer.

"On your bike, you great *******!" said Rosie to her sister.

"You know what will happen if you keep saying that word, don't you?" her sister replied.

"What word?" asked Rosie.

"*******!" said her sister.

"Say that again?" said Rosie.

"*******!" said her sister (again).

"Can't say I do," said Rosie.

"Your tongue will

 d

r

o

p –"

She couldn't say anything else, because her tongue had. Dropped off, that is, just like she had warned it would.[1]

"Bratman," said Rosie. "You are well smart!"

"Bratman!" said Dobbin. "I want my dinner!"

1: Of course, if you try this on your sister and she does actually manage to say: "Your tongue will drop off," you can say: "How come yours hasn't, then, smarty pants?"

TEST YOURSELF!!!! On some typical Mystic Meg predictions.

Here is a list of some typical smart-alec predictions sisters make when they adopt the Mystic Meg disguise. See if you can match them to the appropriate activity of yours:

ACTIVITY	YOUR SISTER'S ADVICE
1 Riding your bike backwards down Corkscrew Hill.	**(a)** You know you'll break out in warts?
2 Riding your bike backwards *up* Corkscrew Hill.	**(b)** Pass me the fire extinguisher, in case you spontaneously combust.
3 Eating a Triple Whoppaburger with french fries, chocolate sundae, three raspberry milk shakes and a gherkin. For breakfast.	**(c)** You need a brain transplant.
	(d) Hide!
4 Drawing an "I luv Eck and Dunce[1]" tattoo on your arm with a biro.	**(e)** You'll end up looking like a grotesque splodge. Not that it really matters because no one will notice.
5 Calling Greebo Grudgesnottle, the class heavy, a "creepy little nerd with the face of a constipated rhinoceros."	

ANSWERS

1 = (e); 2 = (c); 3 = (b); 4 = (a); 5 = (d).

1: The famous drop-dead-gorgeous Geordie boy band.

Sister Disguise 5: **Sister Hood**

A couple of days later, I stood with Mary Goround on her front path, while Dobbin finished eating what was left of the flower bed. Suddenly, something bright and shining flashed past our eyes.

"That's my natty jacket!" exclaimed Mary.

"I didn't know natty jackets could walk," I said.

"It's not walking!" said Mary.

"All right, I didn't know natty jackets could *run*," I replied.

The jacket turned round. "I'm only borrowing it, Mary!" called a voice from inside the natty jacket.

"That's my sister! Wearing *my* jacket!" declared Mary.

"Correction. It's your sister wearing your natty jacket *and* her Joker-type Sister Hood disguise."[1]

"I'm going to call *Crimewatch*!" called Mary.

1: See *How To Handle Your Brother* page 29.

And so she did.

The trouble was, though, that by the time they'd done all their filming and things, Mary's sister – and her natty jacket – were over the hills and a great way off.

"Have you or Dobbin got any ideas?" asked Mary, desperately.

Handling Your Sister's Sister Hood Disguise:

This was Dobbin's verdict:

The only decent sort of jacket is a donkey jacket.

"My suggestion is this," I said. "Stick this notice on your natty jacket."

And so she did.

The next time, Mary's sister "borrowed" her natty jacket, the police caught her, the fire brigade rolled up and turned a hose on her and the ambulance was on hand to take her to hospital (she needed it after Mary had finished with her).

"Thanks, Bratman!" said Mary.

A copy of the note I gave Mary is to be found for your own use on the next page...

THIS NATTY JACKET IS STOLEN!!!!

DIAL 999 IMMEDIATELY AND ASK FOR THE POLICE, FIRE AND AMBULANCE!!!

THANK YOU

TEST YOURSELF!!!! On Sisters' Joker-type Disguises

1 Which famous cartoon film character is a typical sisters' Joker-type disguise?

    (i)   Snow White
    (ii) Quasimodo
    (iii) Dumbo

2 Which famous dog is a typical sisters' Joker-type disguise?

    (i)   Snoopy
    (ii) The Hound of the Baskervilles
    (iii) Spot

3 Which famous film featuring a creature of the oceans is a typical sisters' Joker-type disguise?

    (i)   *Jaws*
    (ii) *Flipper*
    (iii) *Free Willy*

4 Which famous TV personality is a typical sisters' Joker-type disguise?

     (i)   Otis the Aardvark
     (ii) Mystic Meg
     (iii) Budgie the Little Helicopter

5 Which of the following "sisters" is a typical sisters' Joker-type disguise?

     (i)   Sister Sledge
     (ii) Sister Sister
     (iii) Sister Hood

HOW TO SCORE:

1:   If you picked **(i)** don't take any points! In fact, take this book and start at page one again. And this time read it properly. I mean, come off it, Snow White was an innocent, put upon young girl – does that sound like your sister? If anything, your sister's more likely to resemble one of Snow White's Seven Dwarves: Grumpy, probably.

    If you backed your hunch and picked **(ii)** take 1 point. On the other hand, if you hunched your back, I hope you don't mind your name being used in this book, Mr Modo. Only it rang a bell.

    If you picked **(iii)** take no points at all. To say your sister is like Dumbo is an insult. To elephants everywhere.

2: If you picked **(i)** take 1 point.
If you picked **(ii)** take half a point: it probably is very easy to mistake the staring eyes and gleaming white gnashers of the hound of the Baskervilles for your sister's.

GRRRR!

If you picked **(iii)** you'll get a scab.

3: If you picked **(i)** take 1 point.
If you picked **(ii)** you're wrong, wrong, wrong! And if you don't believe me, take a bucket of raw fish, throw them at your sister's face and see how many she manages to catch between her teeth.

If you picked **(iii)** take half a point. It's *wailing* your sister does when she doesn't get her own way, not *whaling*.

4: If you picked **(i)** take -10 points. I mean, if your sister disguised herself as the Aardvark, would anybody be able to tell the difference? If you picked **(ii)** take 1 point.

If you picked **(iii)** take no points. The only person who ever tried to disguise herself as Budgie was Darren Copter's sister, Little Ellie.

5: If you picked **(i)** take ten points for inventiveness. Using your sister as a toboggan is a great idea.

If you picked **(ii)** take half a point – half a point of milk that is. Fix yourself a shake then sit down and watch *Sister, Sister*. Now ask yourself, could your sister *really* disguise herself as the bright, witty, attractive, intelligent star of a TV show?

If you picked **(iii)** take 1 point. Then hide it quickly, before your sister nicks it.

WHAT YOUR SCORE MEANS:

One point: Well smart
Two points: Two smart
Three and a half points: Clever
More than four points: Too clever by half (by half a point that is).

How To Handle Your Sister: Stage Two

BRATMAN AND DOBBIN'S GUIDE TO ESSENTIAL SISTER-HANDLING EQUIPMENT

You should never attempt to handle your sister without first ensuring that you have access to the following vital items of sister-handling equipment:

1: The Brat Mobile

There are, of course, three kinds of Brat Mobile:

1: BRAT MOBILE (a.k.a. Dobbin)

2: BRAT MOBILE

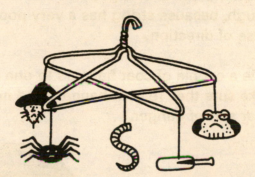

3: BRAT MOBILE

Of these though, only one is the true BRAT MOBILE. Can you guess which one it is? The answer's over the page.

OVER THE PAGE...

ANSWER:

1: This isn't the real Brat Mobile. This is a horse.
2: This isn't the real Brat Mobile. This is a phone-y.
3: This is the real Brat Mobile!

Here's how you make a Brat Mobile:

HOW TO MAKE A BRAT MOBILE

1 Take a piece of string. Don't take it far though, because string has a very poor sense of direction.

2 Tie a couple of coat hangers to one end. Make sure they're coat hangers and not any other sort of hanger.

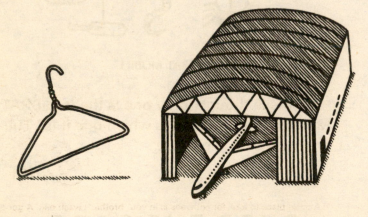

Coat Hanger   Aircraft Hangar

3 Take it into a darkened room.

4 Stick it to the ceiling. Or if you want to make a rather more thorough job, seal it to the sticking.

5 Tie some creepy things on to the coat hangers.
Either by:
(i) Cutting out some creepy things from the next page.
or:
(ii) Finding your own creepy things like cobwebs or spiders' legs, if you know where to look.[1] You could, of course, use the most creepy thing of all, your big sister's boyfriend Sebastian Swott. If you use him, be very careful not to do any damage. To the coat hanger, that is.

6 Now stand back and laugh merrily as your sister walks into the BRAT MOBILE. Scaring herself silly[2].

1: A good place to look for cobwebs is in your brother's wash bag. A good place to look for spiders' legs is on the end of spiders.

2: Mind you, she might not actually scare herself *silly* as the chances are she's pretty silly already.

SPIDER

RAT'S TAIL

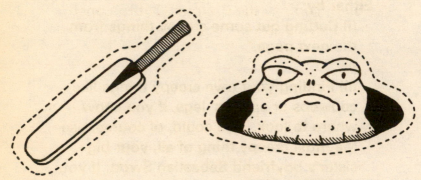

BAT

TOAD (in the hole)

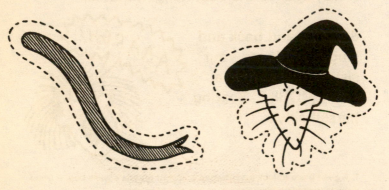

LIZARD'S TONGUE

WITCH'S WHISKERS

BRATMAN AND DOBBIN'S GUIDE TO ESSENTIAL SISTER-HANDLING EQUIPMENT

2: The Bratman Out-to-Lunch Box and the Dobbin Out-to-Lunch Nosebag

Do not confuse the Bratman Out-to-Lunch Box with a Batman Lunch Box:

Batman Lunch Box

Bratman Out-to-Lunch Box

It's called the Out-to-Lunch Box because that's what your sister is most of the time – out-to-lunch. And I don't mean she's round at her best friend Katie's having a Pot Noodle[1]. I mean she's mad, or to put it another way – or rather another five ways – bonkers, crazy, loopy, nutty, two sandwiches short of a picnic[2]. I mean after all, we are talking here about someone who:

– thinks that the girl band Squash are better than Eck and Dunce!

– keeps a three-legged hippopotamus under her pillow.

1: Not that they'd be eating Pot Noodle, anyway. Being completely bonkers your sister and her friend will be eating Completely-Potty Noodles.

2: Not to mention two Mars Bars short of a lunch box. But that's mainly because she and her friend Katie are on diets.

– thinks Glenn Hoddle is a Scottish beauty spot.

The Bratman and Dobbin Out-to-Lunch Box can be used for:

– carrying spare parts for the Brat Mobile.

– carrying a good supply of Bratman Paper Hankies.[1]

– carrying a good supply of mud for putting under your sister's pillow. (Hippopotamuses like mud, don't they?)

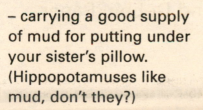

1: See page 43.

The Bratman Out-to-Lunch Box comes complete with a Dobbin Out-to-Lunch Nosebag. This is particularly useful if you want to eat your dinner in peace without having to look at your sister.

On some (thankfully rare) occasions[1], the Bratman Out-to-Lunch Box can be very useful for handling brothers, too.

BRATMAN AND DOBBIN'S GUIDE TO ESSENTIAL SISTER-HANDLING EQUIPMENT

3: Bratman and Dobbin Paper Hankies

See opposite.
One sure way to get up your sister's nose!

1: See *How To Handle Your Brother*, page 35.

!!! Warning !!!

This is the end of Bratman and Dobbin's advice on *How To Handle Your Brother*. The other half of this book contains advice on *How To Handle Your Sister*. Some of the things in this half of the book are very gruesome – mainly the sisters. Do not turn the book round to read it unless you're like Dobbin, i.e. you have the constitution of a horse. You can of course just carry on reading. That way you won't get upset, because all the words will be upside down and you won't realize just what gruesome words they are.

!!! Warning !!!

This is the end of Bratman
and Dobbin's advice on *How
To Handle Your Sister*. If you
want to read the other half of
the book, I should warn you,
there's a lot in it that's ridiculous
and pathetic – that's the descriptions
of the sort of things brothers get up to.
So, I don't really expect you to
want to read it. If you do, I shall
be mightily surprised.
In fact, it will be a turn up
for the books!

5..
....
....

3 BARTERING
(e.g. I'll give you my Eck and Dunce
poster with one corner ripped, if
you lend me your Squash CD.)

1..
....
....

2..
....
....

3..
....
....

4..
....
....

5..
....
....

4...
....
....

5...
....
....

2 INFORMATION I CAN GET FROM HER
(e.g. what the embarrassing thing that
happened to mum when she went on
Guide camp was; who her best friend
Denise Dipsticker really fancies.)

1...
....
....

2...
....
....

3...
....
....

4...
....
....

How To Handle Your Sister: Stage Six

THE BRATMAN AND DOBBIN PRETTY GOOD USES FOR A SISTER FILE

1 THINGS SHE CAN GANG UP WITH ME ON AGAINST DAD  (e.g. definitions of "a reasonable amount of pocket money"; buying a decent 4WD vehicle to replace our embarrassing Montego; persuading him *not* to volunteer for the school dad's football team.)

1..
....
....

2..
....
....

3..
....
....

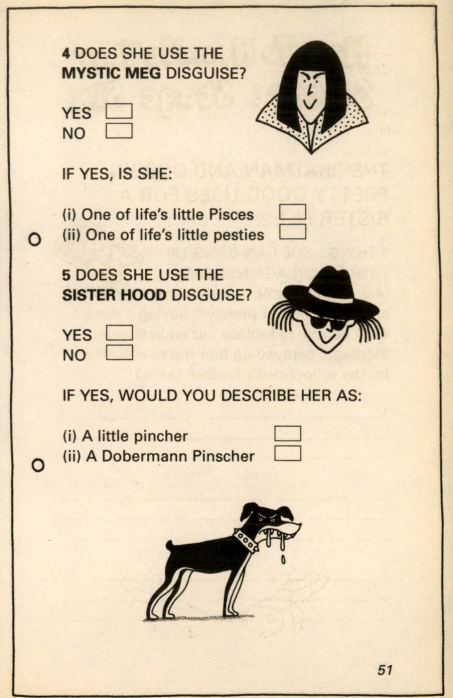

4 DOES SHE USE THE **MYSTIC MEG** DISGUISE?

YES ☐
NO ☐

IF YES, IS SHE:

(i) One of life's little Pisces ☐
(ii) One of life's little pesties ☐

5 DOES SHE USE THE **SISTER HOOD** DISGUISE?

YES ☐
NO ☐

IF YES, WOULD YOU DESCRIBE HER AS:

(i) A little pincher ☐
(ii) A Dobermann Pinscher ☐

3 DOES SHE USE THE **JAWS** DISGUISE?

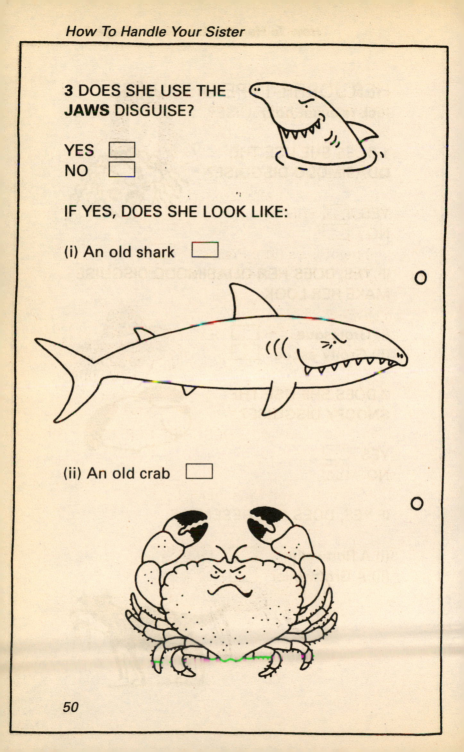

YES ☐
NO ☐

IF YES, DOES SHE LOOK LIKE:

(i) An old shark ☐

(ii) An old crab ☐

HER JOKER-TYPE DISGUISES
(tick relevant box)

1 DOES SHE USE THE
QUASIMODO DISGUISE?

YES ☐
NO ☐

IF YES, DOES HER QUASIMODO DISGUISE
MAKE HER LOOK:

(i) Grotesque ☐
(ii) Grotty-esque ☐

2 DOES SHE USE THE
SNOOPY DISGUISE?

YES ☐
NO ☐

IF YES, DOES SHE RESEMBLE:

(i) A Rottweiler ☐
(ii) A Grottweiler ☐

ANSWERS:

1=(f); 2=(a); 3=(b); 4=(c); 5=(d); 6=(e).

BRATMAN AND DOBBIN'S VERDICT ON YOUR SCORE:

More than 4 right: Wer-hayyyy!!!!

More than 4 wrong: Blurbbbbb!!!!

More than 40 wrong: Would you like to borrow my little brother's *Learn To Count With Postman Pat* video?

One sheep, two sheep, three sheep!

How To Handle Your Sister: Stage Five

THE BRATMAN AND DOBBIN SISTER'S JOKER-TYPE DISGUISE FILE

Draw your sister below.

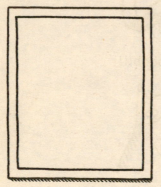

Front view

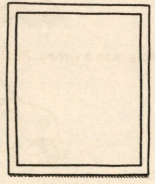

Side view

NAME...

THE AGE SHE IS:.......................YEARS OLD

(FOR OLDER SISTERS) THE AGE SHE TELLS
BOYS SHE IS..................YEARS OLD

1	2	3
lolloping	pong	gurgler
gradely	grot	stencher
poodling	banana	boncer
piffling	sludge	slugger

Practise here:

"You're a
...........1........... ....2...........
with the face of a
..........2.......... ....3..........."

"You're a
..........1.......... ....2..........
with the intelligence of a ....1..........
..........2.......... ....3..........."

"You're a
..........1.......... ....2..........
with the taste of a
..........2.......... ....3..........."

How To Handle Your Sister: Stage Four

CHECKLIST!!!!!
On the finer points of your sister's
Joker-type disguises.

BRATMAN AND DOBBIN'S
~~MIX 'N'~~ MATCH QUIZ:

Match the following sounds with what
makes them:

THE SOUND	WHAT MAKES IT?
1 £$%^&*@!	**(a)** Your *I Was Frankenstein's Monster's Vampire Werewolf* video
2 Yahhhh!	**(b)** Dobbin's verdict on your sister's Quasimodo disguise.
3 Aaargh!	**(c)** Your reaction to seeing your sister's Jaws disguise.
4 Eieieie!!	**(d)** What your sister says in her Snoopy disguise.
5 Hee-hee!	**(e)** What you say when you are suddenly struck – by a thought.
6 Yee-oww!!	**(f)** A very rude word.

How To Handle Your Sister: Stage Three

BRATMAN AND DOBBIN'S FIVE CHART TOPPING INSULTS TO HURL AT SISTERS

Surprise and outrage your sister by using Bratman and Dobbin's unique range of very rude-sounding insults.

Mix 'n' match any one insulting word from column 1 with any insulting word from column 2 and any insulting word from column 3.